HOLLY'S GODLY ADVENTURE

HOLLY'S GODLY
ADVENTURE

By
JANAE LEPIRE

Illustrated by
OLANDO LEE

RESOURCE *Publications* • Eugene, Oregon

HOLLY'S GODLY ADVENTURE

Resource Publications
An Imprint of Wipf and Stock Publishers
199 W. 8th Ave., Suite 3
Eugene, OR 97401

www.wipfandstock.com

PAPERBACK ISBN: 978-1-7252-5808-2
HARDCOVER ISBN: 978-1-7252-5809-9
EBOOK ISBN: 978-1-7252-5810-5

Manufactured in the U.S.A.   March 3, 2020

It was a warm, sunny summer day and Holly wanted to do something fun. Since her little sister, Anya, was sick, mommy had to
stay home with her; because daddy had to work. It would be just
awful to have to waste this wonderful day, though.

Grandma and grandpa agreed with Holly. It would be a great day to do something outside and enjoy the wonderful world God made for His children. So, they picked Holly up and decided to take her on a surprise adventure in the mountains.

Once they reached the mountain road, there were so many things to see as they drove along. Beautiful butterflies were seen around every turn. There were also lovely deer, wildflowers and various small animals that helped make the ride fun and interesting.

Holly and grandma enjoyed looking at all the wonderful sights out the windows. They also had fun pretending that, as the road went up and down steep hills, they were on a big roller coaster. They "screamed" and laughed as they went around big curves and up and over each big hill.

At last Holly and her grandparents reached the visitor center, near the hiking trail to their destination. They went into the visitor center first, so they'd know what to expect along the trail. They were so excited to see all the beauty they knew God had placed there.

As they started out on their hike, they saw more butterflies and some honeybees. After walking along just a short way, Holly heard some water running close by. She walked off the trail just a little, and saw a pretty stream. As she got closer though, Holly saw something in the stream that was more than just water! What do you think she saw?

Holly called to grandma and grandpa to come quickly. There in the stream was a water snake! It was very interesting, but everyone knew not to get to close to it. Holly and her grandparents went back up to the trail as quickly as possible. While they knew that God made all creatures; they realized that some are still dangerous and God always wants us to be careful.

After hiking along a little further, Holly spied the cutest little family of chipmunks. It was so much fun to watch them running around, collecting their acorns and climbing up and down the trees. These were something God had made that they could enjoy watching up close. Although they still knew that you never try to pet a wild animal; no matter how cute they may be or how close you can get to them.

After a few minutes, Holly and her grandparents continued on their hike. Soon they could hear the sound of rushing water and they knew they were getting very close to the end of the trail and the surprise that Holly would find there.

They walked on, carefully checking the rocks they came upon to see if they were sturdy enough to step on. If the rocks were loose, they made sure to go around them, or step over them. They didn't want to take a chance on slipping and getting hurt. At last they came to a section of the trail that led down, down, down. They very carefully, climbed it, until it stopped. Can you guess what beautiful sight Holly saw there?

It was an incredible waterfall. One like Holly and her grandparents had never seen before. As they got closer to it, they could see where there was a "pool" at the bottom. Everyone there had taken their shoes off and were playing in the water! So, of course, Holly and her grandparents did also.

As they looked up, they saw the water falling in several, separate sections from the stream above onto the lovely rocks and down in the "pool" below. It was a truly beautiful sight and playing in the water, there at the bottom of it all, was so much fun. They thanked God for making this incredible place for all of His children to enjoy.

After, what seemed like much too short a time it was starting to get late and Holly's grandparents said it was time to go back. Unknown to them, though, that was not the end of the adventure at all.

 It was a little harder to hike back, since it was mostly uphill, instead of down. Because of all the amazing things they came across though, they really didn't mind, or even notice the climb. The wonder of all God's nature just kept getting more interesting as the day went along.

Suddenly Holly heard something. An unusual noise, from the woods, not far off the trail. As she and grandma held hands and walked off the trail, slightly, to investigate, they couldn't believe what they saw. What do you think it may have been?

There climbing between the trees and over some rocks was a baby bear cub! It was so cute and fun to watch for a few minutes. Then they heard a big roar and knew that the mommy bear was coming. While they would have liked to see her, they knew that would be too dangerous!

So, Holly and grandma quickly met grandpa back on the trail and continued to walk on, thinking the big adventure was over for the day. They were wrong. Can you imagine what else they could have seen?

Holly was walking a little bit in front of her grandparents when, all of a sudden, three very large bucks ran across the trail, right in front of her. It was an incredible sight! They were amazing, beautiful and so fast! They were also so close to Holly that she could almost have reached out and touched them. It was a Blessing that God let them see the bucks so close up, but He didn't let them get close enough to hurt anyone.

Wow! What an incredible adventure this turned out to be. Since they still had a little way to get back to the car, it wasn't completely over yet, either. They still saw more deer, this time some lovely does with their babies, eating in the field along the path. One of the does even watched them and walked the same way that Holly was going, until the woods stopped and they were at the parking lot again.

As Holly and her grandparents got back into the car, they couldn't believe all that had happened. They were a little sad to have to leave. They were also happy, and thanked God, for all they had seen and the wonderful day they had together. Even on their way home, there was more of this incredible world to experience.

When they stopped to look off of the mountain at the lovely valley below, there were rocks to climb. Of course, Holly and her grandparents, again, knew to climb very carefully and never get too close to the edge. It was some extra added fun to end the day though.

There was also still one more surprise to see here also. There, sunning itself on a big rock was a big, black snake. Again, everyone there knew to just enjoy looking at it from a distance and not get too close. Still, though, it was another piece of God's great world to admire.

Let's all try to get out and enjoy the wonderful world that God made for us as often as possible. Don't forget to Thank God for His gift of this amazing and beautiful world and the greatest gift ever, His Son, Jesus Christ!

www.ingramcontent.com/pod-product-compliance
Lightning Source LLC
Chambersburg PA
CBHW071232170626
46809CB00005BA/2045